STAR WARS™

CHAOS AT THE CASTLE

WRITTEN BY NATE MILLICI

ART BY ANDREA PARISI & GRZEGORZ KRYSINSKI

Disney • LUCASFILM PRESS

Los Angeles • New York

D0888189

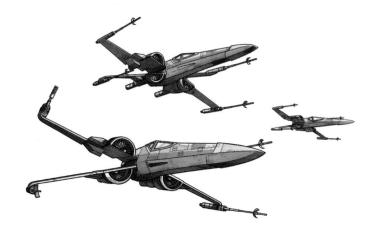

All rights reserved. Published by Disney Lucasfilm Press, an imprint of Buena Vista
Books, Inc. No part of this book may be reproduced or transmitted in any form or
by any means, electronic or mechanical, including photocopying, recording, or by any
information storage and retrieval system, without written permission from the publisher.
For information address Disney • Lucasfilm Press, 1200 Grand Central Avenue,
Glendale, California 91201.

Printed in China

First Boxed Set Edition, October 2016   10 9 8 7

Library of Congress Control Number on file

FAC-025393-22178

ISBN 978-1-4847-9037-3

Visit the official *Star Wars* website at: www.starwars.com.

Rey, Finn, BB-8, Han, and Chewie were on the run from the First Order.

Han knew his friend Maz
could help them.
Maz lived in a castle.

Strange creatures filled the castle.
A First Order spy was also in the castle.

Maz was happy to see her old friend Han.

The little alien gave them a big feast.

But Finn wanted to leave.
He did not want to fight
the First Order.

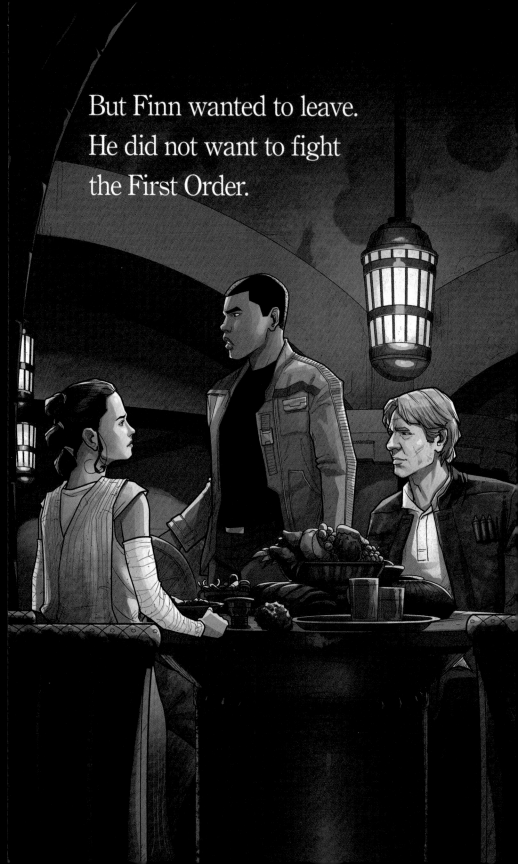

Rey did not want Finn to go.

She was sad to say good-bye to Finn.

Rey walked through the castle.
She went down a staircase.
BB-8 followed her.
Something called to Rey.
It led her into an old dark room.

Rey found an old trunk in the room.
Rey started hearing strange things.

Her mind was filled with pictures
she had never seen before.

Rey opened her eyes.

Maz was there.

Maz said that Rey had felt the Force.

The Force was an energy field.

It could be used for good or evil.

Rey was scared of the Force.
She ran away.

Then the First Order
attacked Maz's castle!

Finn wanted to stay
and help his friends.
Maz gave Finn a lightsaber.

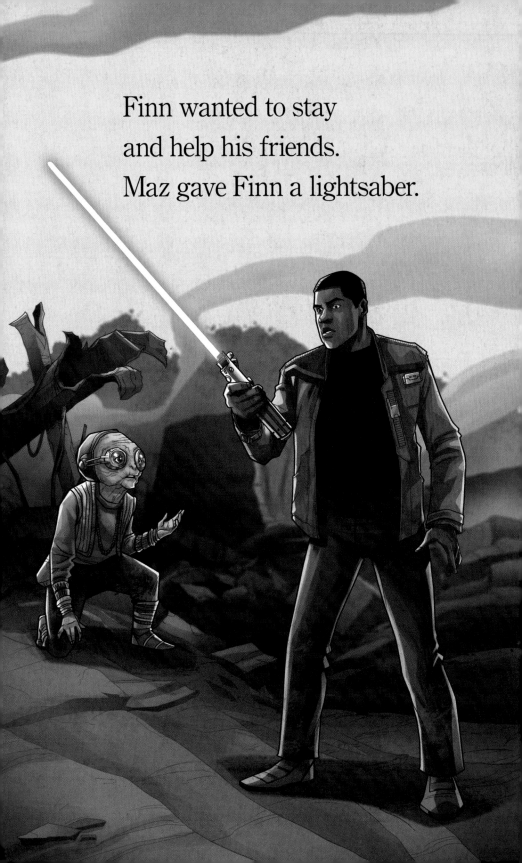

First Order troopers
fired on the castle.

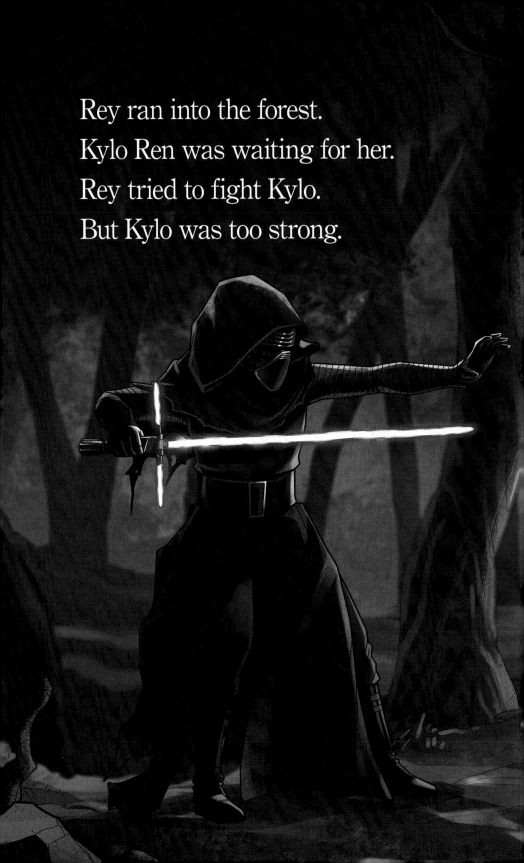

Rey ran into the forest.
Kylo Ren was waiting for her.
Rey tried to fight Kylo.
But Kylo was too strong.

Finn needed to find Rey.
He fought off a trooper.

Han and Chewie fought off
troopers, too.
But they needed help.

The Resistance flew to the rescue!
X-wing fighters raced toward
the castle.

Poe and the other pilots fought the
First Order ships in the sky.

But Kylo captured Rey.
He took her to his ship.
Then the ship flew away.

The battle was over.
Another ship landed.
Leia walked out!

Leia was the leader of the Resistance.
Leia took the heroes back to her base.

Now the team could make plans
to save Rey.
Their new mission was about
to begin!